Meg Parker and the Look Alike Mystery

Eleanor Robins

High Noon Books
Novato, California

Cover Design and Illustrations: Herb Heidinger

Glossary: afternoon, wonder, wig, voice.

International Standard Book Number: 0-87879-441-7

3 2 1 0 9
0 9 8 7 6 5 4 3 2

Contents

CHAPTER 1

Meg Wants To Help

Meg went into the kitchen. Her mom and her little sister Amy were making a cake. There was a lot going on.

Meg said, "Is there anything I can do to help, Mom?"

"I'm helping Mom. She doesn't need your help," Amy said.

Her mom said, "I can always use more help, Amy. And there is something Meg can do for me."

"But I want to help you by myself," Amy said. She didn't look very happy.

Her mom said, "I don't want Meg to help us with the cake, Amy. I have something else she can do for me."

"What, Mom?" Meg asked.

Her mom said, "You can take a book to Miss Miller for me. I told her I would give it to her after I read it. You can take it now. Or you can wait and take it later."

"I'll go on and take it now. Miss Miller might be in a hurry to read it," Meg said.

Miss Miller and her mom were good friends. Miss Miller lived in a very big house. And she had a lot of money.

"Where is the book?" Meg asked.

"It's on the table in the hall. I'll get it for you," her mom answered.

"That's OK, Mom. I'll get it," Meg said.

Meg went into the hall and got the book. Then she went back into the kitchen.

"Did you find the book, Meg?" her mom asked.

Meg said, "Yes, Mom. It was right where you said it was. I'm going to call Kate before I go. She might want to go with me."

Kate, Meg's best friend, lived just across the street.

Meg walked to the phone and called Kate. Kate answered on the first ring.

Kate said, "Hi, Meg. I was just thinking about you. And I was getting ready to call you. What are you doing this morning?"

"I'm getting ready to take a book over to Miss Miller. Do you want to ride over to her house with me?" Meg asked.

"Sure. Are you going right now?" Kate asked.

"As soon as I can. Do you want to meet me at my car?" Meg said.

"OK. Let me tell my mom. Then I'll be right over," Kate said.

"I'll see you in a few minutes," Meg said.

Meg hurried into the kitchen. She told her mom where they were going.

CHAPTER 2

The Girls Get a Surprise

Kate was coming across the street when Meg went outside. Both girls quickly walked over and got in Meg's old green car. Then Meg backed out of her drive.

"How long are we going to stay at Miss Miller's house?" Kate asked.

"Not very long. Why?" Meg asked.

"Do you think we'll have time to stop by the Ice Cream Shop? You know how much I like ice cream," Kate said.

Meg said, "Yes, I know how much you like it. And sometimes you like it too much. We can stop by the Ice Cream Shop. But Dave and Fred won't be there."

Dave was Meg's boy friend. And Kate liked Fred a lot. Both boys worked at the Ice Cream Shop.

"Are you sure they won't be there?" Kate asked.

Meg said, "I'm sure. Dave told me they wouldn't be at the Ice Cream Shop at all this morning. But they will be there this afternoon."

"Then let's wait and go there this afternoon. I can wait for some ice cream," Kate said.

Meg stopped her car in front of Miss Miller's

house. She and Kate got out of the car. They quickly walked to Miss Miller's front door. Meg was carrying the book.

Meg rang the door bell. But no one came to the door.

"I don't think anyone is here," Kate said.

"Miss Miller must be here. Her car is in the drive. Maybe no one heard the door bell. I'll try again," Meg said.

Meg rang the door bell again. A few minutes later she rang it another time.

"Let's go, Meg. I told you no one is here," Kate said. She started to walk away.

Meg said, "Wait, Kate. I think I saw someone looking out the window at us."

Meg rang the door bell again.

After a few minutes the thin woman who lived with Miss Miller opened the door.

Meg said, "Wait, Kate. I think I saw someone looking out the window at us."

"Hello, girls. What can I do for you?" the woman said.

"Why didn't you come to the door sooner? Didn't you hear the door bell?" Kate asked.

"No, I didn't. This is a very big house. And I was busy in the kitchen. I'm sorry you had to wait," the woman said.

"That's OK," Meg said.

"What can I do for you?" the woman asked the girls again.

"We came to see Miss Miller. I have a book for her," Meg answered.

"I'll take the book. You can't see Miss Miller right now," the woman said.

"Why can't we?" Kate asked.

The woman didn't look pleased. She said, "Miss Miller fell and hurt her leg. She can't walk to the door."

Meg said, "I'm sorry to hear that. We'll be glad to go inside and take the book to her."

Kate said, "I see Miss Miller. She's sitting in the living room."

Kate pushed past the thin woman and hurried into the living room.

The thin woman's face turned red. She said, "Come back here. Miss Miller doesn't feel like seeing you right now."

The thin woman hurried after Kate. Meg hurried after both of them.

Kate walked over to the woman she thought

was their friend Miss Miller. She said, "Hello, Miss Miller. We hope your leg is better soon."

Then Kate got a good look at the woman. She was very surprised.

Meg walked over to Kate. She got a good look at the woman. Then she was very surprised.

The woman looked a lot like their friend Miss Miller, but she really wasn't their friend.

CHAPTER 3

Another Miss Miller?

Kate said, "You aren't Miss Miller. Who are you? Are you Miss Miller's sister?"

"Yes, I am," the woman answered.

The thin woman's face still looked very red. She said, "She's come here to stay while her sister has a hurt leg. Her name is Miss Miller, too."

Meg said, "My name is Meg Parker. And this is my friend Kate Brown. We're very glad to meet you."

"I'm very glad to meet you girls, too," the

other Miss Miller said to them.

Meg looked very carefully at the woman. There was something about the woman that wasn't quite right. But she didn't know what it was.

The woman said, "I'll be glad to give the book to my sister."

"Thank you," Meg said. She gave the book to the other Miss Miller.

Kate looked very carefully at the other Miss Miller. She said, "You sure do look a lot like your sister. Someone who didn't know her well would think you were our friend Miss Miller."

The thin woman said, "You have to go now, girls. I'll walk with you to the door."

The thin woman quickly walked with the girls to the door. Then she almost pushed them out the door.

The girls started walking back to Meg's car.

"She sure did seem in a hurry for us to go," Kate said.

"I know. I wonder why," Meg said.

Meg turned around and looked back at Miss Miller's house. The thin woman was looking out the window at them.

"That's funny," Meg said.

"What is?" Kate asked.

"That thin woman is looking out the window at us. She must want to make sure that we're really going," Meg said.

The two girls got in Meg's car. Meg started driving away. Kate looked back at the house.

"Meg, that woman is still looking at us," Kate said.

"I wonder why," Meg said.

For a few minutes the two girls didn't say anything. They were both thinking.

Then Meg said, "I never heard Miss Miller say she had a sister."

"I have a brother. But I don't go around telling people I do," Kate said.

"That's not the same thing," Meg said.

Meg kept thinking about the other Miss Miller. There was something about the woman that wasn't quite right.

CHAPTER 4

A Loud Voice

It wasn't long before the girls were back at Meg's house. Meg parked her car in the drive. Then the girls got out of the car.

"Do you want to come in for a while, Kate?" Meg asked.

"Sure. It's still a long time before lunch," Kate said.

The girls went inside the house. Then they walked into the kitchen. Meg's mom and her little sister Amy were washing dishes.

Meg's mom told Kate that she was glad to see her. Then she said, "How was Miss Miller?"

"She fell and hurt her leg. She can't walk for a while," Meg answered.

"I'm sorry to hear that. I wish there was something we could do for her," Meg's mom said.

"I know something we can do, Mom," Amy said.

"What?" her mom asked.

"We can give her the cake we made. And we can make another one for Dad," Amy said. Amy liked to make cakes with her mom.

"That's a very good idea, Amy," her mom said.

"Yes, Amy, it is," Meg said.

"Meg, can you take the cake over to Miss Miller right now?" her mom asked.

Amy said, "I can't go with you. I have to help Mom make another cake for Dad."

"I sure can," Meg said.

Her mom walked over to get the cake. Then she gave it to Meg. She said, "Be sure to tell Miss Miller that I hope she feels better soon."

"I will. Do you want to go with me, Kate?" Meg asked. She forgot to tell her mom that she and Kate met Miss Miller's sister.

"Sure," Kate answered.

Amy said, "I can't go with you. I have to help Mom make another cake for Dad."

Meg didn't tell Amy that she wasn't planning to ask her to go with them.

Meg and Kate hurried back outside to Meg's car.

"I'll hold on to the cake," Kate said.

The girls got in the car. They were glad they could do something to help someone.

Meg looked up and down the street. Then she backed out of the drive. Kate was holding the cake.

It wasn't very long before they got to Miss Miller's house.

Meg and Kate got out of the car. They started walking to the front door. Kate was carrying the cake.

The girls heard a woman's loud voice. The woman said, "You won't be able to get away with this. The police will find out before you can get out of town."

CHAPTER 5

The Girls Talk to Miss Miller

Kate said, "I think that was Miss Miller's voice. I wonder what's going on in there."

"We'll soon find out," Meg said.

Quickly Meg rang the door bell. But no one came to the door.

Meg kept ringing the door bell. She wasn't going to go away before someone came to the door.

Meg saw the thin woman looking out the window at them. She rang the bell again.

A few minutes later the thin woman opened the front door.

The woman looked mad. She said, “What do you two girls want this time? I told you Miss Miller can’t see you. She isn’t feeling well. And she needs her rest.”

“We have a cake for her. And we want to see her. We want to be sure she’s all right,” Meg said.

The woman said, “How can she be all right? You two girls keep ringing the door bell so she can’t get any rest.”

“We heard what Miss Miller said,” Kate said.

The woman looked funny. “What are you talking about? What did you hear her say?”

"That the police would find out about something before someone could get out of town," Kate said.

Sometimes Meg wished that Kate wouldn't tell everything she knew.

The woman said, "You didn't hear Miss Miller talking. You must have heard someone on TV talking. Wait here a minute. I'll go see Miss Miller. Maybe she feels like seeing you for a few minutes. Then you'll know she's all right."

The woman closed the door.

"What do you think, Meg? Do you think we heard someone on TV talking?" Kate asked.

"Maybe we'll get to see Miss Miller. Then maybe we'll know who was talking," Meg said.

A few minutes later the thin woman opened the door. She said, "You can come in and see Miss Miller. But you can't stay very long."

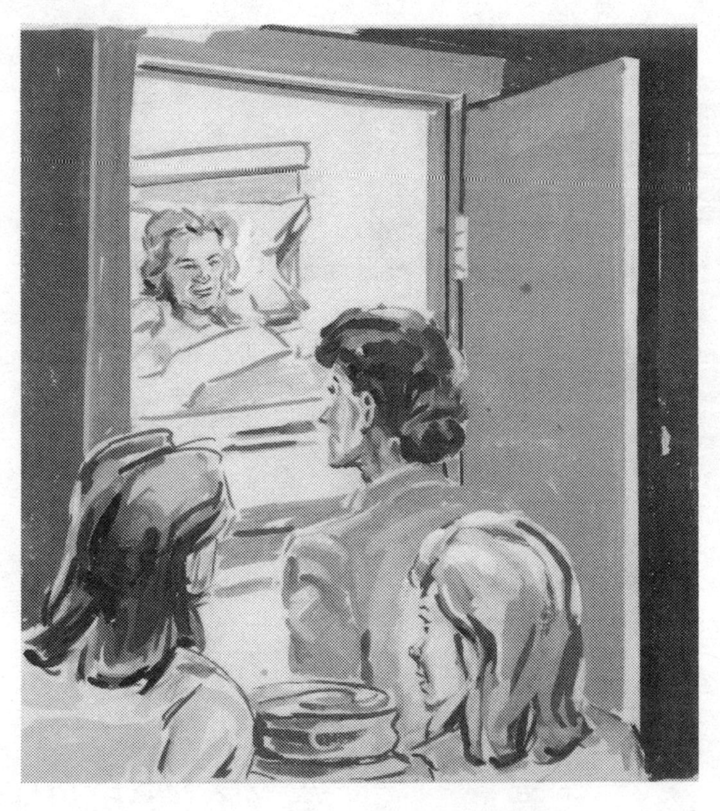

The two girls followed the woman to Miss Miller's bedroom.

Meg and Kate hurried inside the house.

"Follow me," the thin woman said.

The two girls followed the woman to Miss Miller's bedroom. Kate was carrying the cake.

Miss Miller's sister was next to the bed.

The thin woman said, "Miss Miller, these two girls are worried about you. They want to be sure you're all right. I told them that you fell and hurt your leg. They thought they heard you talking before they rang the door bell. I told them they heard someone on TV talking."

Miss Miller didn't look well. She said, "I didn't know my TV was on so loud, girls. I'm sorry you're worried about me. I did fall and hurt my leg. But I'll be all right soon."

Meg looked over at the TV. It was turned off. But some people turned their TV off when someone came to see them.

Meg said, "My mom sent you a cake. She said to tell you that she hopes you feel better soon."

"Thank you for bringing me the cake. Tell your mom I said thank you. Now I must ask you to go. I must get my rest," Miss Miller said. She looked like she wished the girls would hurry and go.

Her sister said, "Don't forget that you wanted to tell your friends who I am."

Miss Miller said, "That's right. I'm sorry I forgot. Girls, this is my sister. She's come to stay with me while my leg is hurt. She will be a big help to me while she's here."

The thin woman walked over to Kate. She said, "Give me the cake. I'll put it on the table for Miss Miller. Then I'll walk with you two to the front door."

The woman took the cake from Kate and put it on the table. Then she walked with the girls to the front door as quickly as she could.

She opened the door for the girls. Then she said, "Come back next week to see Miss Miller. I'm sure she'll feel much better then."

She almost pushed Meg and Kate out the door.

CHAPTER 6

A Trip to the City

The girls started walking to Meg's car.

Kate said, "I'm glad we got to see Miss Miller. We must have heard someone on TV talking about the police."

"I hope you're right, Kate," Meg said. But she wasn't sure Kate was right.

"I must be right. Why would Miss Miller have been talking about the police?" Kate asked.

Meg said, "I don't know. But first you told the woman we heard Miss Miller say something about the police. Then the woman let us inside to talk to Miss Miller."

Kate said, "I must have been wrong about thinking I heard Miss Miller say that. It must have been someone on TV. Miss Miller didn't act like she needed the police. And the thin woman said we could come back next week to see her."

"I know. But next week is a long time off. But you're right about one thing. Miss Miller didn't act like she needed the police," Meg said.

The girls got in Meg's car. Meg looked back at the house. The thin woman was looking out the window at them.

Meg drove away. It wasn't very long before the girls were back at Meg's house.

Kate said, “I’ll be back over after lunch.”

Kate started walking across the street to her house.

Meg hurried inside her house. She walked into the kitchen. Her little sister Amy was still helping their mom.

Amy said, “I’m glad you’re back, Meg. There’s something else you can do to help Mom.”

“What?” Meg asked.

“Yes, Amy. What can Meg do to help me?” her mom asked.

“A man from the store called while you were gone, Meg. My new dress has come. You can drive into the city and pick it up for me. Then I can wear it tomorrow,” Amy said.

"Meg may have something else she wants to do this afternoon," her mom said.

"Meg, you never do anything for me," Amy said.

Meg knew Amy liked to forget all the things she had already done for her. But she didn't tell Amy that.

"Amy, I'll be glad to get your dress for you," Meg said. She was always glad to drive into the city.

"Thanks, Meg. Sometimes you're OK to have for a sister," Amy said.

Her mom said, "Meg, you're using all your gas doing things for me. I'll give you some money so you can buy some more gas."

"You don't have to do that, Mom," Meg said.

Her mom said, "But I'm going to anyway. Your dad and I said you had to pay for your own gas. But you don't have to when you're using your car to do something for us."

Meg hurried to call Kate. Both girls were very excited about going to the city.

The girls left for the city as soon as they could after lunch. It was a long way to the city. But it didn't seem like a long way to them.

Meg saw a place to park next to the store.

"I'm glad we won't have to walk far," Kate said.

"So am I," Meg said.

CHAPTER 7

Something is Wrong

Meg and Kate hurried inside the store. Then they quickly walked over to a man who worked in the store.

The man gave Meg a box with Amy's new dress in it. Then he said, "Aren't you from the same town as the rich Miss Miller is from?"

"Yes, we are," Kate said.

The man said, "She's here now buying many new dresses. We hadn't seen her in a long time. I'm glad the woman with her told us who she is."

"Where are they now?" Meg asked.

"Over there," the man answered. Then he showed the girls where the two women were.

Then he showed the girls where the two women were.

Meg and Kate saw the thin woman. But the woman with her wasn't their friend Miss Miller.

"She's Miss Miller's sister," Kate said.

Meg had a feeling that something was very wrong. Then she thought of something her mom had told her a long time before.

Meg said, "Kate, I just thought of something."

"What?" Kate said.

"Mom told me that Miss Miller said she didn't have any brothers and sisters. So that woman can't be her sister," Meg said.

"Then who is she? And why did she say she was Miss Miller's sister?" Kate asked.

"I don't know," Meg answered.

The two women walked out of the store.

"Come on, Kate. Let's follow them," Meg said.

The girls hurried out of the store. They followed the two women for a few minutes. Then they saw the two women go inside a bank.

"Why are they going in a bank?" Kate asked.

"I don't know. But we're going to try to find out," Meg answered.

The two girls hurried inside the bank after the two women. But the women didn't see them.

The two women walked over to a man who worked in the bank.

The thin woman said, "This is Miss Miller. I

told you that she would be in today."

The man said, "Come with me. I'll have the money for you in just a few minutes."

The two women went with the man.

Meg said, "Now I know what's going on. They're trying to get Miss Miller's money. We knew that woman wasn't Miss Miller. That's why she told us she was Miss Miller's sister. But everyone in the city thinks she really is Miss Miller."

"What are we going to do?" Kate asked.

"I'm going to call Uncle Bob," Meg said.

Meg's uncle Bob was her dad's brother. He was also the Police Chief in their town.

CHAPTER 8

The Girls Help Miss Miller

Meg hurried to a phone. She called her uncle Bob. She told him all about taking the book and the cake to Miss Miller. She told him all about what the man in the store said. And she told him that the two women were in the bank to get some money.

Her uncle said, "Stay at the bank, Meg. I'll call the police in the city. They'll come over there and find out what's going on. I'll go to Miss Miller's house. Then I'll call you at the bank."

"Thanks, Uncle Bob. I knew you would know what to do," Meg said.

Meg hurried over to tell Kate what her uncle Bob said. The girls stayed in the bank so he could call Meg back.

It wasn't very long before two policemen hurried into the bank. They quickly walked over to a woman who worked in the bank. They asked her where they could find the woman who said she was Miss Miller. The woman told them. Then they hurried into the room where the two women and the bank man had gone.

A few minutes later the policemen came out with the two women. The thin woman was yelling at the policemen.

The other woman no longer looked as much like Miss Miller. Her gray wig had come off. The girls could see that she was really a young woman. She had made up her face to look like an old woman. Then Meg knew what hadn't seemed quite right about the woman.

The policemen and the two women left the bank.

Then the bank man came hurrying out of the other room. He walked over to Meg and Kate. He looked at Meg. He said, "Are you Meg Parker?"

"Yes, I am," Meg said.

"Come with me. Your uncle Bob wants to talk to you," the man said.

Meg and Kate followed the man into the other room. Meg picked up the phone.

Meg said, "Hello, Uncle Bob. Did you find out anything about Miss Miller? Is she all right?"

Meg's uncle said, "The woman who lived with her locked her in her room. But she's fine now. She said to tell you that she didn't have a hurt leg. And she said to tell you it was her voice you heard this morning."

"Why didn't she tell us that when we saw her?" Meg asked.

"The woman who lived with her made her say what she told you. The woman said she had to tell you that or the woman would hurt you and Kate," Meg's uncle said.

"Tell Miss Miller that Kate and I are glad she's all right," Meg said.

Meg's uncle said, "I'll be glad to tell her. But she wants you two girls to come to see her later this afternoon. She wants to thank you for stopping the women from taking her money out of the bank."

"We're glad we could help," Meg said.

Meg put the phone down. Then she told Kate and the bank man everything her uncle had said. The bank man thanked the two girls for all their help. Then the two girls left the bank and walked back to Meg's car.

It didn't seem very long before the girls were back in their town. Meg drove over to Miss

Miller's house. Miss Miller thanked the girls. She wanted to give them some money for helping her. But the girls wouldn't take the money.

She wanted to give them some money for helping her.

The girls went back to Meg's car.

Then Kate said, "Now we can go to the Ice Cream Shop. I sure would like some ice cream."

"We're on our way there now," Meg said.

Soon the girls walked into the Ice Cream Shop. They sat down at a table.

Dave came over to them. He said, "What have you two been doing today?"

Kate said, "Ask Fred to come over so we can tell him, too."

The girls told the boys all about taking the book and the cake to Miss Miller. And they told them all about going to the store and to the bank.

Then Meg said, "The best part was being able to help Miss Miller."